Whales Passing

by EVE BUNTING

illustrated by

LAMBERT DAVIS

THE BLUE SKY PRESS
An Imprint of Scholastic Inc. • New York

For Tracy Taylor Bunting —E. B.

For Lachlan and Connor — L. D.

THE BLUE SKY PRESS

Library of Congress catalog card number: 2002003371

ISBN 0-590-60358-2

10 9 8 7 6 5 4 3 2 1   03 04 05 06 07

Printed in Singapore   46

First printing, May 2003

Designed by Kathleen Westray

My dad and I

stand in the scratchy grass at the cliff's edge

and watch the whales go by.

There are five.

"A pod," my father says.
"They're orcas, every one.
They may have come from colder seas
where icebergs float and break.
Icebergs, blue-white and polished by the sun."

I watch the drifts that are their breaths . . .

. . . and then they dive,
deep, deep among the streams of fish
and star-dance light
that fills their sea.

"How do they know which way to go?" I ask.

The sea is the same each way I turn,

and the sky is empty, too,

except for pelicans,

a kite-tail string of them across the blue.

"I bet those whales have signposts down below.

An ocean mountain

or a sunken ship.

Maybe another whale that tells them, 'Follow me!

We'll make a right

at this white rock.'

That is, if whales can talk."

My father smiles.

"Of course they talk.

They story-tell

each day they swim, from here to there

and farther still.

They whistle

and make clicking sounds

and squeal.

"They say a baby orca hears its mother's voice before it's born into the sea."

"And answers back?" I ask.

"Maybe."

We stay and watch them surface, spout, and dive.

We watch until they disappear.

All five.

I wonder if the whales saw us?

"That was a boy," one whale would say.
"He and his dad will surely talk of us
and how they saw us pass.
The small one's shirt was red
as sunset on the sea.
His shorts sky blue.
His socks blue, too."

"They lack our blubber, sad to say.

But humans have no love of fat.

Imagine that! No love of fat!"

Car-ee! Car-ee!

The high whale laughter
screeches through the sea,
and other whales join in.

"No need to laugh," the first whale says.

"Those humans have their place, and we have ours."

"The thing is well arranged," a small whale says.

She leaps a frolic leap and slaps her tail.

Soon she will have

her first-born calf,

and she is filled with joy.

The whales think of the boy

and he of them.

"My dad and I saw whales,"

I'll tell my mom.

"They saw us, too.

I wonder, when they talk down there,

do bubbles bubble up?"

"You think they talk?"

My mom will smile.

"Of course they do," I'll say.

"But not like you and me."

They're gone.
My dad and I will come again

and see the whales.

For now I'll hold this shell

I found close to my ear

and hear the sea.

And I'll remember

whales passing.

ABOUT ORCAS

Orcas are also called killer whales, and sometimes they are called wolves of the sea. Of course they are not wolves, and they are not true whales either. They are actually dolphins—the largest members of the dolphin family.

Orcas are beautiful, sleek creatures, black above and white below, with a white patch over each eye and a white saddle in front of their dorsal (back) fins. Males can be up to twenty-seven feet long and weigh up to eleven tons. That is heavier than many African elephants. Female orcas are slightly smaller. Most orcas travel in pods (packs), which are groups of killer whales. A pod is a kind of whale family, and its members usually stay together for life.

Orcas like to eat seals, sea lions, big and little fish, and even other whales—often ones bigger than themselves. Their favorite snacks are the tongues and lips of other whales. Their teeth are large and cone-shaped. They are set alternately in the upper and lower jaws so that when they close, they snap together like a trap. Luckily for us, orcas have never been known to attack a human.

A killer whale can live as long as thirty-five years. Scientists can tell the age of a dead whale by counting the layers on its teeth. That is similar to the way naturalists count the rings on a tree stump to see how old the tree was when it died.

An orca can swim at speeds up to thirty miles an hour. Its tail flukes move up and down and push it through the water. Its flippers guide it in the direction it wants to go. It has one nostril (blowhole) on the top of its head that closes when the whale is underwater. When it surfaces, the orca lets out its breath in a giant "whish" which makes a cloud called a spout. A spout looks like a fountain and can be very high. The blubber (fat) under the orca's skin is very thick and keeps the whale warm even in the coldest water.

Killer whales are travelers and are found in every ocean in the world as they look for the best food spots. While they swim, they "talk" to one another and to distant pods, calling out in clicks, whistles, and screams. Orcas can see quite well, even in murky water, but they depend more on their incredible hearing. They use the sounds they make themselves to bounce off schools of fish or underwater obstacles. The sound echoes back. If it comes back quickly, the whale knows the object is close. If it takes longer, it knows the object is still far away. This system is called echolocation, and it is also used by some kinds of bats to navigate in the dark.

We have learned so many things about killer whales, but there are many things we don't know. What do they think about as they cruise our deep oceans? What do they talk about? We can only use our imaginations. Killer whales are mysterious, as are all sea creatures, living in a watery world so different from ours. Orcas are not a threatened species. They are so fierce and so fast that they have no natural enemies in the ocean. And although they are large, commercial whalers consider them small whales. They are small, compared to the blue whale (one hundred feet long) or the fin whale (eighty-seven feet long). To whalers the orca is not worth taking. But the pollution in our oceans is now a risk to all sea creatures. We can hope that we will stop polluting. And that the beautiful orcas will travel safely in our oceans forever.